For Ellie and Douglas
V. C.

First published 2014 by Walker Books Ltd
87 Vauxhall Walk, London SE11 5HJ

This edition published 2015

2 4 6 8 10 9 7 5 3 1

Text © 2014 Jeanne Willis
Illustrations © 2014 Vanessa Cabban

The right of Jeanne Willis and Vanessa Cabban to be identified
as author and illustrator respectively of this work has been asserted
by them in accordance with the Copyright, Designs and Patents Act 1988

This book has been typeset in Cochin
Printed in China

British Library Cataloguing in Publication Data:
a catalogue record for this book
is available from the British Library

ISBN 978-1-4063-6005-9

www.walker.co.uk

WALKER BOOKS
AND SUBSIDIARIES
LONDON • BOSTON • SYDNEY • AUCKLAND

Emily Peppermint's
TOY SCHOOL

JEANNE WILLIS

illustrated by

VANESSA CABBAN

"Welcome to Toy School everybody!" said Emily Peppermint. "Who can tell me what we'll be learning today? Hands up."

"I haven't got any hands!" said Shmoo.

"Miss? Miss! Are we going to learn how to do our hair
  like a princess?" asked Edie.

"I haven't got any hair!" said Tinny Tim.

"The reason you are here is to learn all about children," said Emily. "Because one day, you will belong to a child."

"What is a child?" asked Gumbo. "Do they have four legs, little horns and long necks?"

"Do they growl when you tip them upside down?" said Little Ted.

"No two children are
alike," explained Emily.
"But they all begin
as babies."

"That one's pinned together,"
  said Little Ted.
"That's a nappy," said Emily.
"Babies wet themselves."
"I wish I could wet myself," said Edie.
"Plastic dolls can. Are babies made of plastic?"

"Babies aren't made like toys,"
explained Emily.
"They're born and grow
into children."

"Grow?" gasped Edie. "If I grew,
my knickers wouldn't fit!"
"You forgot to put them on,"
said Gumbo.

Just then Rose, who helped Emily
in the classroom, came in pushing
an enormous pram.

"Park the pram on the rug, please," said Emily. "Then the toys won't get hurt when I teach them how to fall out of it."

Rose handed out the safety helmets.

"Miss, why do we have to wear funny hats?" asked Little Ted.

"If you gather round, I'll explain," said Emily.

"If you belong to a baby, you might
get thrown out of the pram."

"Aghhh!" panicked Shmoo. "I don't want to belong to a baby. Babies are bad!"

"Babies aren't bad," said Emily. "Remember our school motto: **Good toys make good children.**

"When a baby throws you about, it's just being playful. As a good toy, you just have to play along.

"Rose will now demonstrate the correct way to land."

One by one, the class practised falling out of the pram.

"Gumbo, keep those knees tucked in," said Emily.

"I can do roly-polies,"
said Shmoo.
"Wheee…!"
"Duck!" called Emily.
"Who me?" said Rose.
"No, look out!" said Emily.

"Now, let's go outside
and practise without
the rug," said Emily.

"It's a lovely day for being
thrown out of a pram,
isn't it?" said Rose.

Everyone followed Emily onto the field.

"Climb in, Class," said Emily. "When I call your name, fling yourself out as if you'd been thrown by a great big baby."

"Off we go…"

and the pram began
to roll down the hill …

with all
the toys inside it…

"Oh no!" shouted Emily.

"Run, Rose!"

"I've got a stitch," said Rose.

"Several stitches actually.

My side seam has come undone."

"Peepers porkers!" gasped Emily. "They're heading for a muddy ditch!"
But just as she had almost caught the pram handle, it hit a rock and …

... all the toys
flew out.

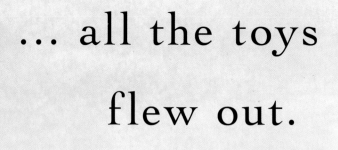

SPLAT!

"Don't worry, Miss!" said Gumbo. "We landed perfectly."

"I've got a screw loose," bleeped Tinny Tim.

"That's nothing new," said Edie.

Back in the classroom, Emily Peppermint announced
the next lesson. "Children need clean toys," said Emily.
"This afternoon, I'm going to teach you
how to swim …

"… in the washing-up bowl.

Who wants to go first?"